MW00987955

MURDER ON A CRUISE SHIP

P. CREEDEN

Murder on a Cruise Ship © 2019 P. Creeden

Edited by Marcy Rachel

All rights reserved under the International and Pan-American Copyright Conventions. No part of this book may be reproduced or transmitted in any form or by any means, electronic or mechanical, including photocopying, recording, or by any information storage and retrieval system, without permission in writing from the publisher.

This is a work of fiction. Names, places, characters and incidents are either the product of the author's imagination or are used fictitiously, and any resemblance to any actual persons, living or dead, organizations, events or locales is entirely coincidental.

Warning: the unauthorized reproduction or distribution of this copyrighted work is illegal. Criminal copyright infringement, including infringement without monetary gain, is investigated by the FBI and is punishable by up to 5 years in prison and a fine of $250,000.

Hear about P. Creeden's newest release, FREE books when they come available, and giveaways hosted by the author—subscribe to her newsletter:
https://www.subscribepage.com/pcreedenbooks
All subscribers also get downloadable copy of the PUPPY LOVE coloring book.

MURDER ON A CRUISE SHIP

Ridgeway Rescue Mysteries can be read in 1-2 hours. Perfect for when you're waiting for an appointment or just want a fast read. Don't miss out on this quick, clean, cozy mystery that will keep you guessing until the end!

All hands on deck! It's a beautiful spring day and 20-year-old Emma Wright is meeting her crush, Colby Davidson, for a two-hour tour specifically for dogs and their owners – *The Canine Cruise*. She and Molly, the Saint Bernard, are so excited to see both Colby and Gabby, his K9 partner, as the two have been away on training.

It's smooth sailing until someone shouts "man overboard!" A news reporter who is covering the day cruise for a local station falls into the fast-flowing

Potomac River, and she doesn't know how to swim. Did the reporter fall overboard in an accident, or was it murder?

I t was silly for Emma to feel so giddy while driving from Ridgeway to Potomac, Virginia, but she couldn't help herself. She spied Molly, the Saint Bernard puppy, sitting in the back area of her SUV. The puppy had been a rescue and a foster, and Emma had been training for Molly to become an emotional support dog, which had been going better than most expected from the six-month-old puppy. To train her properly, Emma had been introducing Molly to several different environments. Most businesses would let the service-dog-in-training enter their establishments as long as she wore her red vest, and they'd been going to dog parks and other animal-friendly environments to get the Saint Bernard used to the sights and smells of different animals, and not allow those things to distract her from her job as a therapy dog. And that was what the trip to the nation's capital was about today.

So, why did Emma feel so giddy?

Colby Davidson and Gabby, the German Shepherd, were coming on this foray as well. Emma smiled to herself as she hummed along with the radio. She'd been smitten with the K9 deputy for as long as she could remember. And just as long as she could remember, he'd treated her as a kid sister. With a sigh, she pushed those thoughts out of her head. She was dressed especially cute today for the "Canine Cruise" that they were taking down the Potomac River. She wore a simple sundress with a sweater and tights. The weather had been unseasonably warm in Ridgeway, but she knew Virginia could host three seasons at once across the state on any particular day in April. She hoped she wore enough to stay warm.

Her father, the sheriff of Ridgeway, had sent Colby up to D.C. for a conference and training camp specifically for K9 cops. His training session was almost over, but he had the weekend to relax and do whatever he pleased. Emma had internet-searched the area thoroughly for an excuse to come visit him and stumbled upon the cruise. The two-hour long

"Canine Cruise" was a great opportunity to introduce Molly to a boating environment and allow the puppy to see new sights. And the almost three-hour car ride also introduced Molly to long distance drives. Everything fell into place when Emma had told her dad about the cruise and how she was going to drive up Saturday for the sake of training Molly. Her father suggested that she call Colby, just as she hoped he would.

She pulled into the parking lot, excited as the gravel popped under her tires. Several cars parked in straight rows, following the painted lines over the rocks. She peered through them, looking for the familiar K9 Police SUV from Ridgeway, wondering if Colby might already be at the docks. Emma let out a slow breath when she didn't see his vehicle. It was no big deal. She was a little more than fifteen minutes early, excited for the cruise and the prospect of seeing Colby, since he'd been away from Ridgeway for almost two weeks and would be gone from home for one more after their "date" today.

No, it wasn't a date to Colby.

But Emma liked to think of it that way, since they would be spending time together... had made an appointment to spend time together... without her father or any of their friends from Ridgeway present at the event. When she opened her car door, the salty breeze brushed against her cheeks, and made her reach back in the car to grab her jacket off the passenger seat. The balmy April air caused a shiver to run through her body, and goose flesh to rise on her arms. Over toward the docks, a few barks and yips carried on the wind toward her. The sound of the other dogs made Molly stand on her feet in the back of the SUV, her ears perked toward the river.

"There's a good girl," Emma said to Molly as she snapped the leash onto Molly's harness and then pulled the tailgate down on the back of her SUV. She gave Molly a big scratch behind the ears, but Molly wasn't interested in affection as much as casting her drooping gaze toward the continued din from the dock area. Molly lifted her nose and sniffed the salty breeze. Nothing in Ridgeway quite smelled of the sea like it did here in Potomac.

"Can I give you a hand at all?" a deep baritone asked from behind her.

Emma's heart leaped a bit in her chest when she thought it might be Colby, but when she turned around, she was face to face with an unfamiliar, blond-haired, blue-eyed man with a crooked smile who was about ten years her senior, and had a Jack Russel Terrier on the end of his leash. She couldn't

4

help the way her heart sank toward her stomach but tried to school her features so that the disappointment wouldn't show. She smiled up at him. "Thank you for the offer, but Molly is a good girl, even though she's already seventy-three pounds. Luckily, I don't have to pick her up and place her on the ground anymore, or I'd be in trouble."

He chuckled at that.

Then Emma spied the K9 Police car she'd been waiting for as it crunched gravel. Colby sat in the front seat of the car and smiled her way as he pulled in one of the spots near her. She'd purposefully chosen an area of the lot that had empty space all around in the hopes that she'd make it easier for him to find her.

"I'm Steve Shaw, by the way," the man in front of her said, offering a hand for her to shake.

She blinked at him and then realized what he'd said and moved the leash to her left hand so that she could take his hand in a shake. "Emma Wright."

At the same moment, Molly realized that there was a new friend low to the ground and hopped down from the SUV to rush over and greet Steve's Jack Russell Terrier. Steve laughed. "And this is Roscoe. He loves big dogs, especially the females."

This was exactly the kind of situation that Emma

was hoping to find herself in, to test Molly the puppy's ability to overcome stimuli and behave the way she'd been trained for the past month and a half. In a stern voice, Emma said, "Molly, sit."

Without a moment to spare, Molly's haunches came down and she looked up at Emma. Emma couldn't help but smile at the pup. But the moment of obedience came to a quick end, as Molly's front end collapsed as well and she was down, low to the ground, playing roughly with her new friend, Roscoe. Emma sighed. It was a lot to ask of such a young puppy to behave perfectly the first time they went on an outing with so many other new dogs present. For now, Emma would have to find herself happy with small victories.

"Emma!" Colby's voice called out, and her heart fluttered in her chest.

She beamed a smile his direction as he stepped over toward her. It wasn't often that she had the chance to see him in something other than his police uniform, but he stood there in plain blue jeans and a Virginia college sweatshirt. Light brown curls peeked out from under his police ball cap. His green eyes sparkled at her, and then he turned toward Steve Shaw, his brow furrowing slightly.

Colby stuck out a hand the man's direction. "Colby Davidson."

The man chuckled nervously and put out his hand. "Steve Shaw. A pleasure to meet you, officer."

Colby nodded. "Are you here for the Canine Cruise as well?"

Steve nodded and smiled at Colby, nervously glancing at the hat on Colby's head. Emma watched the interaction, feeling badly for the man who'd stop to ask her if she'd like help. Like a typical police officer, Colby tended to sound as if he interrogated people rather than just making friendly conversation. After suffering through a few more questions, Mr. Shaw made his escape. "Well, I guess I'll see y'all aboard the cruise. Pleasure meeting you both."

"Thank you," Emma said and then glanced up at Colby who continued to watch the man leave. Then she looked down at Colby's side and frowned. "Where's Gabby?"

Colby finally pulled his gaze from the man walking away from them and met eyes with her. "She's in the truck. I was just making sure that guy wasn't giving you any trouble. You really shouldn't let yourself be so open with strangers. You never know when someone might be a danger to you.

Keep your senses sharp and don't be so quick to trust everyone who approaches you."

He was worried about her? She couldn't help but smile a bit at the thought. Together they went to the back of his SUV to let Gabby, the German Shepherd, down. The two of them fell into pleasant conversation. Colby told her a bit about how the boot camp was going, and Emma let Colby know how things were going back in Ridgeway without him. *Lonely*, she wanted to say, but held her tongue on that bit of knowledge. Then the two of them started toward the pier and the cruise ship waiting at the dock. Emma couldn't help but feel her heart swell that Colby would be all hers for at least the next two hours.

CHAPTER TWO

The cruise ship was much bigger than Emma thought it would be for just a two-hour jaunt on the Potomac River. The deck had three floors, the top one open to a dramatic view of the shorelines while the bottom two were mostly indoors with large windows looking out in both directions. The main floor, where they boarded was the second-floor area. On this main deck of the ship, there were several booths where people with dog-friendly services had set up shop. Emma spotted a groomer, a canine manicurist, and even a dog whisperer doing psychic readings. Colby huffed a laugh when he pointed in the direction of the psychic, and how her booth seemed to be the busiest among the other people aboard for the cruise.

Several people came in pairs, often with one dog between them, but some of them had two dogs, just like she and Colby. A very pretty woman stood in a bright red suit dress with a microphone in her hand, speaking energetically to the man holding a large video camera. "We're here today for our Monday Pets' Spotlight, coming to you from Potomac Cruise's Canine Cruise. On the last weekend of every month, the cruise line allows for dog owners to come aboard with their favorite canine companion. The cruise hosts several different contests, including best picture with the Washington Monument, best behaved, and most friendly. We'll interview some of the contestants throughout the cruise tour, and bring you interviews with the winners. Stay tuned!"

"And cut!" a man off to the side of the camera said, as he straightened the lapel of his brown suit jacket, his glasses shining in the sunlight overhead. "That was excellent, Melinda."

She smiled, but it looked strained. And the cheerful energy she had a moment before settled into a worried look as the man next to the camera came closer.

Emma and Colby were passing by them both when the man said in a quiet tone, "I just wanted to give you a warning about what I heard, so you wouldn't be surprised. It's a childish prank. Also, I need to talk to you what you did to my younger brother, but right now we have a show to shoot. When this cruise is over, we need to have a conversation."

Emma glanced at the woman whose eyes went wide as she backed away from the older, larger man in the brown suit. Even though Emma didn't know what was going on between the two of them, there was no mistaking the sound of contempt in the man's voice. She tightened her hold on Molly's leash and then peered over at Colby, but Colby seemed preoccupied with showing the worker on the cruise our tickets. Emma swallowed down her anxiety for the woman. The man had said that they would talk about it later. He wasn't in a passionate state, but a rational one. The woman wasn't likely in danger. Emma just needed to relax about it.

And it didn't take long for Emma to get distracted by everything that was happening on the cruise ship. A professional obedience trainer had a small, fenced off section that allowed owners to work on their simple obedience commands. On the lowest deck, they had an area with a short wall surrounding it for owners to allow their dogs to play off-leash. Even Gabby stood with her nose up and wagging her tail, fully acting as though she realized that today was all about play and not about work.

Emma's stomach lurched as the ship began to pull away from the port. A cheer went up and the crowd began to clap. The two of them clapped with the crowd. Colby and Emma followed their noses to the gourmet dog treat stand, where the lady gave out free samples of her wares.

"What a lovely pair of dogs," the woman said with a wide smile. "You two are lucky to find love with someone who's also a dog a lover. My husband prefers cats."

Heat rushed to Emma's cheeks, and she shot a glance at Colby. She didn't mind being mistaken for a couple with her crush, but she'd hate if he felt uncomfortable with the prospect. But Colby didn't react or correct the woman. He just smiled back and asked, "Are these biscuits made with any egg products?"

"The peanut butter flavor and the lamb and rice flavor have no egg products. All the biscuits are made with all-natural ingredients, and I tried to make them in a variety of flavors to help accommodate dogs with common allergies. They are also made with top shelf ingredients, so they are safe for human consumption, as well," she said and took a bite out of the cookie in her hand. Then she laughed. "Although they are a little bland for us, since they are made with very little salt, and no sugar."

Relieved after the awkward moment passed, Emma laughed and asked, "We actually live in southwestern Virginia. Does your bakery have an online store?"

The woman's eyes sparkled. "Yes. We have a store through our website. The business card attached to each sample treat baggie will give you all the information you need to order more treats if you'd like."

Colby took one of the sample baggies and handed it to Emma, and then took a second one for himself. "Peanut butter is Gabby's usual favorite, so if she's keen on these, I may come back and buy a bigger bag at the end of the cruise. I just don't want to carry much for the next two hours."

"Actually, if you decide you like the cookies early on, you can avoid the last minute crowd by placing an order with me before we come back to port. I'll reserve your cookies off to the side," the woman said with a wink.

"Thank you." Colby shortened up Gabby's leash a bit and guided Emma away from the booths with a hand on the small of her back. Once they were a few feet away from the gourmet treats, he turned to her and asked, "Is there any particular plan you have in mind?"

She shrugged. Just getting him here was her plan, and his hand momentarily on the small of her back heated her up and sent electricity coursing through her body. That, all by itself, made the whole trip worth it. Finally, she answered, "The trip is about two hours long, so I definitely want to give Molly a bit of puppy time, off-leash in the play area. But right now, let's go to the upper deck and get some pictures with D.C. in the background. I hear they have several good scenes set up for people, too. Maybe we'll get something good enough to put in the contest."

He laughed. "Even if we don't it will make a good memory."

Her heart fluttered at the thought that Colby might want to keep this day in his memories, too. She swallowed it down, trying not to get too excited or too ahead of herself. He only considered her a friend or little sister. People make good memories with family members and friends just as often as they do their dates. It was nothing to get too excited about. But that didn't stop her heart from stuttering again when Colby's hand returned to the small of her back as he guided her toward the stairway to the upper deck.

The upper deck was everything that she'd hoped it would be. On the left hand, or port side, several people already stood in line to take photos with the different scenes of tinsel and flowers there. Wind blew strongly on the upper deck, and much of Emma's hair flew into her face. She reached in her bag quickly to find a hair tie and then pulled her hair back in a quick ponytail.

Colby eyed her and smiled. "I like your hair down, but you look good that way, too."

Emma's cheeks burned, and it wasn't entirely from the wind. Did Colby know he was making her feel this way? She wondered sometimes if he meant to flirt with her, but then he rubbed the top of her head, like he would a little kid and pointed toward an area for photos that had just opened up, and she remembered again what she meant to him. Trying to hide the disappointment that pricked her heart like a thorn, she handed the photographer her phone and stepped over toward the display of white roses.

"Everlasting love," she whispered to herself as she touched one of the delicate flowers and sat at the bench.

Colby sat next to her on the bench, his thigh

touching hers as the crowded close together for the photographer. The two of them got Molly and Gabby to sit close together as well, and then smiled for the cameras. The photographer took three photos with each of their phones and then handed the phones back to Emma and Colby. They each swiped through their phones to view the pictures. Colby looked so handsome in each of them, and Emma couldn't help but take note of how they both looked so much like a couple. She peered over at Colby, and saw that the smile on his face had remained unchanged. When he lifted his gaze, his green eyes met hers with joy in them. "Let's go over there to take another—"

But he didn't get a chance to finish his words before there was a loud bang. They looked over in time to see confetti fly through the air. Someone shouted, "Watch out!"

The hairs on Emma's arms stood on end as confetti dispersed in the breeze. The news crew stood on the other side of the top deck, and the reporter in the red dress slipped over the side and out of sight. Her scream was cut short by a splash.

CHAPTER THREE

For a moment, Emma sat frozen, trying to make sense of what she'd just seen, but Colby didn't suffer from the same sense of shock. He shoved his phone and Gabby's leash into Emma's hands and rushed to the other side of the ship.

"She can't swim!" the cameraman yelled.

And the man in the brown suit turned toward one of the ship's crew members. "You need to stop the ship."

Finally, Emma reached her feet, but her knees felt weak again as she watched Colby dive over the railing. A scream lodged itself into her throat. The water was too cold. It was barely spring. He'd freeze. And they were practically three stories up. The dive itself could kill him. Dread settled over Emma like a wet blanket. The woman might have died from the fall, but Colby might also die from trying to save the reporter.

"Man overboard!" someone shouted.

She blinked as she heard the low hum of the engine of the ship die off and the vessel drew to a slow stop. She rushed to the back of the boat, but to do so, she had to wait behind several others who were rushing down the set of metal stairs that lead to the main deck. Her heart pounded in her chest, and she already felt the prayer murmuring on her lips. "Please be okay. Please be okay."

She flush of guilt overcame her as she realized she was only thinking of Colby. After chiding herself, she pictured the red-dressed reporter in her mind also as she continued to send out her prayers for their safety. One of the crew members threw a life preserver over the side of the boat while the man wearing a captain's hat stood nearby talking to the Coast Guard on the radio.

"He's got it!" someone yelled.

He? That had to be Colby, right? Emma squeezed both leashes in her hands and pulled the two dogs closer to her. Both Gabby and Molly looked up at her in response. She nodded to them, saying in a shaky voice, "Everything is going to be okay."

It was more for herself than for their benefit, but Emma really needed to believe he'd be alright.

"He let go again!" a person yelled.

"No," Emma whispered, rushing to the side of the ship, both dogs jogging beside her. The scene played out before her. Waves rushed in what seemed like all directions. The Potomac River was just shy of a mile wide at this point, and the fast moving waters made it difficult to navigate for the best of swimmers. The bright orange flotation device bounced in the waves, pulled by Colby's arm as he swam toward the heap of red dress several yards away from him. The reporter stayed still on top of the water, face down, submerged. "She's not moving," Emma whispered.

The captain of the vessel came up beside Emma and stood next to her at the railing. Emma's eyes remained fixed on the woman for several moments, willing her to move, but she didn't. Colby reached the motionless woman and pulled her face from the water. He pushed her onto the flotation device as a siren horn blared on the other side of him. A coast guard vessel had just arrived, the crewmen already throwing more life preservers and lowering a small boat into the choppy waves. A small measure of relief relaxed Emma's shoulders as they pulled both the woman and Colby aboard the small boat and wrapped them each in a blanket. Emma swallowed and reached down to bury her hands in both dogs' fur coats again. "He's alive. He's fine. Colby's okay."

But her heart remained in her throat. The breeze picked up and licked the sweat from her forehead. She shivered and wrapped her arms around herself. How could she be sweating when she felt so cold? The woman in red remained unmoving, but the rescuers performed CPR on the deck of their vessel. Eventually they stopped, and one of them called to the ship's captain on the radio.

"Rescuers got to both people in time, but one of them is in critical condition. We will need to rush her to shore and get her to the hospital as fast as possible, but the sheriff's deputy wants to return to your ship to investigate this, so we're sending him back over in our John boat. Will you be able to receive him and two officers?"

The captain clicked the button on the side of the radio. "10-4, we're ready to receive them."

Emma's heart pounded as she watched the smaller boat rush over the choppy waves with Colby aboard. The main Coast Guard vessel's flashing lights continued as it rushed past their ship and the small one, from a safe enough distance not to disturb the smaller boat in its wake. The captain of the cruise ship nodded to a crew member and the two of them started off to the stairs to the lower deck. Even though some measure of relief had come over Emma, she still felt too anxious to just sit on the deck to wait. She needed to come. Clutching both leashes in her hands, she rushed after the captain as fast as Gabby and Molly would allow.

Just when she reached the stairwell, a crew member stopped her. "Ma'am, I'm afraid we can't let you below deck at this time. Official police business. No passengers allowed past this point."

"But the sheriff's deputy who jumped into the water... he and I are... together. We boarded the ship together." The tension rose in Emma's chest as she sputtered out the words.

The crewman lifted an eyebrow at Emma. "Are you a family member?"

Her lips pursed. A lie sat on the tip of her tongue, and all she had to do was push it out, but her hesitation was enough of an answer for the crewman.

He shook his head. "Please step back and stay with the rest of the passengers."

Shaking her head, Emma pressed a hand to her chest. Molly pulled on the leash and yanked the hand away, bringing Emma back from the panic attack that had been building in her chest. The Saint Bernard looked up at her with a wagging tail. Gabby sat, a stoic, well-behaved statue, waiting for Colby's return. But the two of them helped Emma get a hold of herself. If she didn't have to care for them both, maybe she'd have time to panic and give in to her anxiety, but as it was, she needed to stay strong. She had to take care of the two of them until Colby returned.

The strong breeze continued to blow, making more people head inside the second floor deck to avoid the breeze. Even the vendors began to put their wares away, as anything that wasn't heavy enough to bare the push of the wind went flying across the deck. Emma's eyes trained back toward the third deck, up top. Would the sets for pictures still be upright, or would they all be blown about by the wind? And if the reporter's fall in the water had been more than an accident, would any clues to the culprit blow away as well?

Without a second thought, Emma started marching that direction with both of the dogs in tow. When she reached the top of the steps, she found the top deck empty of people. The wind had ripped off portions of the picture sets and tossed them into the river. Already they sat, tattered and forgotten by the crew in the melee that had followed the woman's fall. To Emma's right, she found that the deck gate that opened and let the reporter slip through continued to bang in the wind, metal clanging against metal.

Emma pushed her fists into her pockets, leather leash still wrapped around each hand. The last thing she needed to do was contaminate evidence. To keep herself from touching anything, she usually clasped her hands behind her back, but while holding the leashes, it would be nearly impossible to do so, but her pockets were the next best thing. Leaning forward, she peered at the gate and its catch. There didn't seem to be anything defective about either side of the latch, but underneath, she noticed that the gate was triggered by a foot catch which needed to be stepped on in order to open the latch. Was it possible that the reporter had stepped on the latch accidentally?

Colby and Emma had not been too far away at the time. Although Emma hadn't been looking specifically in the direction of the reporter, she tried to bring to mind all of the things that she could recall of the moments before the incident, knowing there could be a clue hidden in the periphery of her vision. She remembered what it looked like when they had finally peered in the direction of the reporter. What had made them even look that way, since she didn't scream until she was falling? There was the bang of a confetti cannon and then a shout. Someone had shouted for the reporter to watch out. Emma stepped closer to the door. If the latch had been keeping the door in place as it should have been, it wouldn't be visible that it was broken or set open. The metal bars aligned with each other, as did the wooden railing at the top. So, how did the person know that there was something to watch out for? Unless...

Unless they wanted to be sure to draw attention to the fact they were trying to stop the reporter from falling while they stood at a distance. They already knew that the door was going to swing out under the reporter's weight. They were trying to take the attention off themselves. Emma's blood ran cold. Chances were good this wasn't merely an accident. And if it wasn't an accident, it was murder.

CHAPTER FOUR

Emma's heart beat wildly in her chest while
the sea breeze blew her pony tail across her
eyes. After putting both leashes in one hand again,
she swiped the hair away from her eyes and
crouched down to study the locking mechanism on
the railing door. She shoved her hands back into her
pockets, one leash in each, to keep herself from actually touching any of the evidence. A black mark
smudged on the white paint around the catch.
Somehow, the door latch was set in such a way that
the door would swing open the moment someone
leaned against it, but otherwise it had to stay aligned
with the rest of the railing to entice someone to
lean there.

But how did the culprit set it up so that the

reporter would be the one to take the fall? Any number of passengers or crew members could have walked past this section of railing and even leaned against this spot. Was it possible that the person who set this up didn't care who got hurt in the process? If they had a specific target in mind, like the reporter, how would they be able to set this up quickly, just before they knew the victim would be here, or keep other people away from this spot until the right moment in time? And then there was the confetti gun. Who had set it up to shoot at the reporter while she stood in this spot, making her fall off balance like that?

"There you are," a deep voice said near Emma's ear, causing her hairs to stand up on the back of her neck. She tensed, but slowly turned toward the sound of the voice, relieved to find Colby knelt beside her. She'd been so wrapped up in her imagination, that she hadn't noticed him approach. Instead of the college sweatshirt and the K9 police officer cap he'd been wearing earlier, he wore a plain blue rugby shirt and a white cap. The ends of his brown hair curled, still wet from his sudden swim in the Potomac.

Gabby stood, wagging her tail and rubbing her head against his leg in greeting.

Emma's heart leapt in her chest. Something about seeing him in a new way made her breath quicken. She swallowed and stood. "I'm not entirely sure this was an accident. Do you remember that someone shouted before she fell? They told her to look out. But if this gate was closed as it should have been, it wouldn't have been a visible problem. No one should have been able to tell that it would open under her weight."

Colby lifted a brow, nodded and looked at the gate himself while taking hold of Gabby's leash from her hand. She handed him his phone as his brow furrowed. "You're right about that. And if the gate had been ajar, certainly, one of the crew members milling about would have seen it."

He narrowed his eyes at the gate as if it offended him and then knelt down to inspect the foot latch, just as Emma had done.

Emma took a deep breath. "What do you think that black mark might be?"

"It's possible that it's the scuff of a shoe. Possibly black shoe polish, or the rubber wearing off from a black sole," he said, just as a commotion started behind them.

The two crew members who wore Coast Guard uniforms stood at the entrance to the top deck, keeping people back. One of the crew members of the cruise ship peered past him, wringing her hands. Fly-aways from the woman's bun whipped around her face. "Can we not at least clean up the mess on the port side of the ship? We won't be very close to the place where she fell."

One of the Coast Guard crew members shot a glance toward Colby. Colby shook his head slightly, stood and came over, offering the female cruise ship member a slight smile. "I'm sorry, but right now this is a potential crime scene. We haven't determined yet whether it was an accident or foul play."

Her eyes formed wide circles, and her voice went up an octave. "Foul play? You mean someone might have done this on purpose?"

Colby shook his head. "No, ma'am. Please remain calm. We don't yet have any evidence to that, but we need to rule out the possibility. Until then, this is an active crime scene, and we can't allow potential evidence to be contaminated."

The woman's eyes remained wide as she nodded slowly and stepped down.

"Did your crew set up the confetti canon?"

She nodded. "It was supposed to go off only when the winners from the contests were announced. I'm the only one who has a remote to it, so I don't know why it went off just before the accident happened."

Colby nodded slowly. "Okay, we'll be down in a few moments."

After staring for another moment at both Colby and the scene behind him, she turned about and ushered the other cruise ship members back down with her. She had stared at Emma for a long moment before turning about, probably wondering if Emma was another police officer or not. Emma swallowed and looked up at Colby as he turned around. He could kick her out of the area along with the rest of the crew, but everything in his body language said that he wanted her to stay.

Colby knelt down next to the confetti canon to inspect it as well. "Did you see anything else out of the ordinary, Emma? Or remember anything?"

She racked her brain. Not only did she want to be useful to Colby, but she wanted the injured reporter to get justice if there was foul play involved. "There were two men with the reporter, right? A cameraman and a director or manager or something. I think we should talk to both of them. Maybe we can get more info." For a moment she chewed on her bottom lip, remembering another small detail, but not sure if she should mention it or not. Finally, she said, "I think I heard one of them saying something like 'I know what you did to my younger brother' and saying he wanted to talk about it later."

Colby blinked hard and snapped his fingers as the two of them stood. "The man in the brown suit. I heard him say the same thing as we were passing by. The color had drained from the reporter's face when he said that. It's very possible that could point to motive in a situation like this. Smart thinking, Emma."

Heat rushed to Emma's cheeks. It was an awful situation to be proud in. Someone had been injured badly and could possibly even die. This was, most likely, attempted murder. Although she didn't know which of the two men, the cameraman or the man in the suit had said to watch out, she also recalled that one of them had said she didn't know how to swim. That would be another detail a murderer would know about the victim in this kind of situation, if he'd set up the accident.

She shivered at the thought. Premeditated murder attempts were shiver-worthy and gave her the creeps. One of her hands automatically sought to bury her fingers into the fur on the back of Molly's neck to find comfort there. Even though she understood that not all of humanity had the same morals and values she'd been raised with as a sheriff's daughter in a small town, she couldn't understand the mindset of someone who set out and planned to kill someone. Overhead, dark clouds began to gather, and a chill added to the already cold breeze. Colby's warm hands grasped her shoulders. "I think we should head to the deck below. There are no more clues here, but maybe we'll find something when we interview the two suspects."

Emma nodded and allowed Colby to guide her to the stairs. Both of the two Coast Guard crewmen eyed her. She could only guess what they thought of her and the way that Colby allowed her to be a part of the investigation. The elder of the two Coast Guard crewmen leaned in toward Colby and whispered in his ear. Colby's frown deepened as he listened and then he nodded and said, "Let's keep this between us for right now. I may need to use this info for leverage in questioning the suspects."

The crewman nodded, and they started down the steps.

Emma gripped the leather leash in her fist and started down the metal stairs to the deck below. Colby opened the door for her as they headed into the crowded play area where many of the dogs had been let loose from their owners to be allowed free time. Barking ensued while owners spoke loudly to one another over the din. The captain of the ship and his crew members spotted Colby right away and headed over toward him. The captain's brow furrowed. "Is there anything more that we can do? I know that crew mates would like to clean up the top deck before any rain, and we'd also like to head back to port if that's okay?"

Colby glanced at the digital time on his smart-phone then lifted a brow at the captain. "How far are we from port, time-wise?"

"Just a little shy of an hour."

Colby nodded. "Start heading back. And the crew mates may clean up the top deck, but stick to the port side, and stay away from the starboard, so that if this turns out to be a crime scene, any clues stay as uncontaminated as possible."

The captain's frown deepened. "Is there anything else?"

"Yes, actually. I need to question the two people who were with the victim, but it's too noisy in here. Is there someplace quieter?"

The captain nodded and pointed to a door at the other end of the enclosed portion of the ship. "You can use the staff manager's office. It's the one with the sign that says, 'employees only.'"

Over by the dog play area, both the cameraman and the man in the brown suit stood together, nervously glancing their direction.   When Colby approached them, the brown suited man stood and came closer. "Thank you for jumping in before and rescuing our Melinda. Do you know if she's going to be all right?"

Colby's jaw tensed and his brow twitched as he answered, "She's stable for now, but unconscious."

Emma's heart clenched in her chest as she read her crush's tells. Colby had lied.

CHAPTER FIVE

"I'm not one hundred percent convinced that this isn't more than an accident, but we need to be sure," Colby said to Emma quietly as they stood just outside the staff manager's office. He swallowed and looked both directions. "For now, come with me and watch the culprit's response. I'll be introducing you as part of the sheriff's department in Ridgeway, just as I am, so go along with it."

Emma nodded, eyes wide. Colby had always been one of the most honest people around, but this would be the second lie he'd told in such a short period of time. She swallowed hard. He had to have good reason, so she just needed to trust him. After taking a deep breath, they entered the room where the brown-suited man and the cameraman both sat on one side of the wooden table. The man in the suit stood. "What is going on? Why are we being questioned if this is an accident?"

Colby shook his head and motioned for the man to sit back down. "If nothing else, you both are witnesses. We will need to see the footage you all recorded and get your personal statements about what exactly happened."

The man's jaw tensed as he sat back down on the bench slowly. Colby motioned for Emma to have a seat while he also sat. Gabby, ever stalwart, already sat at his feet, ready to work whenever Colby demanded it from her. As Emma sat on the bench opposite from the men being questioned, she gave Molly the silent commands to sit, but the Saint Bernard just stood, tail wagging, wanting to see the men on the other side of the table. With a gentle tug on the leash and a tap at the base of her tail with Emma's finger, Emma made her command just a little stronger, but still silent. Molly complied and sat her haunches down. Colby showed both of the suspects that his phone was set to record the conversation before sitting down.

"Let's start with defining your relationship with the victim," Colby offered and then nodded to them both. He pushed a pad and pen in Emma's direction. "Your names for the record?"

Emma picked up the pen and prepared to take notes.

"I'm John Truman, producer of the slice-of-life segment for *News on the Potomac*, and this is our cameraman, Sean Rockfort." The man in the brown suit gestured toward the younger man holding a camera with a red ball cap pulled low over his eyes.

Colby nodded. "Did either of you know the victim well?"

They both nodded, and then Mr. Truman leaned with both hands on the table. "Melinda is a hard woman. You were either on her good side or her bad side, any given day. And if she was feeling especially moody, you might end up on both in one day."

Emma frowned. "That doesn't sound like a very nice description."

The man in the brown suit lifted a brow. "She wasn't, what anyone would call, a very nice person."

Emma blinked at that, holding the pen poised so it was ready to write something down, but she remained unsure what to write but their names. Colby cleared his throat. "So, the victim had a lot of people who didn't like her very much, then?"

The man shrugged. "You could say that."

"How about you, John? Did you like Melinda?" Colby asked, point blank.

A distinct twitch shimmied the man's brow as he forced his smile to remain in place. "Not particularly."

"Did you not like her enough to kill her?"

The man's brow furrowed. "Murder? Are you asking if I could murder Melinda?" He blinked. "No. There's no way I would stoop low enough to kill her. I wouldn't ruin my life in that kind of way. It's bad enough the woman ruined my brother's life. I wouldn't dare let her ruin mine like that."

Colby chewed his bottom lip for a half-moment before asking, "What do you mean exactly? What kind of relationship did the victim have with your brother?"

Mr. Truman's Adam's apple bobbed in his throat as he swallowed. "They dated, briefly... or had an affair, I should say. My brother is married."

Emma barely contained a gasp as she wrote down what she heard and kept herself from peering up at the men as they spoke. Suspects being questioned about delicate matters were better off forgetting she was there so they could share pertinent info with the deputy.

"And what happened to your brother?" Colby asked, leading him to continue.

"He and his wife are currently separated. Last night, his wife tried to commit suicide. They have a daughter less than a year old..." Mr. Truman's voice cracked. "It's a terrible thing. Anita is in the hospital now, too, fighting for her life."

The man had gotten choked up and didn't seem able to continue for a moment. Emma peered up in time to see him swipe his hands at his eyes. The camera man had remained silent the whole time, and from her now seated position, Emma was able to see that his eyes were wide and fixed on the table in front of him as though he was just as distraught as the man talking.

Colby let out a slow breath. "Then it seems you may have a motive if it turns out that foul play was involved in this accident."

The man gasped, his eyes wide as he shook his head. "No way. I told Melinda I wanted to talk to her after the shoot. Talk. I'm not a violent man. There's no way I'd hurt her like that. Besides, that would give Sean more of a motive than me."

Emma frowned as Colby asked, "What do you mean?"

"Anita is Sean's sister."

The hairs on Emma's arms stood on end as goose flesh rose on her skin. Sean had stayed quiet the whole time, but suddenly looked up and shook his head. "No, don't let him pin this on me. I just run the camera. You can check the recording on it. I wasn't anywhere near her at the time. There was no way that I pushed her off the boat."

Colby gestured for the man to sit. "Stay calm. No one is accusing anyone of pushing the victim off the boat. Both Emma and I were on the deck when the incident happened. We know there was no one within ten feet of the victim at the time when she fell. It didn't seem that anyone pushed her. But we did find that the door on that section of the ship's railing appears to be tampered with. We'd like to find out who tampered with the gate and who is responsible for the confetti gun."

"Huh," Mr. Truman huffed and looked toward the cameraman. "I'm not usually one to go around snitching on others, but it would be bound to come out, regardless. I'm sorry, but I overheard you talking about it. The confetti cannon was set up by Sean. He's the one who set it to go off right then."

Sean's face turned beet red as he shook his head. "It was a joke. She wasn't supposed to fall overboard. She was supposed to fall toward the camera, face first. She's just so full of herself, and mean. My sister's in the hospital, and Melinda didn't so much as apologize for her part in that situation. She didn't care. I wanted to embarrass her on camera, that's all. I didn't expect her to fall overboard or get hurt. I just wanted her to get surprised for a moment and lose her composure on camera."

His words rang true, and the man wrung his hands in front of him on the table. It explained his inability to make eye contact since the situation started, but now his pleading eyes were fixed on Colby. Colby frowned. "How did you get access to the remote?"

The man shook his head again, but this time, his gaze didn't shift at all. "I didn't have access to the remote. This slice-of-life segment was my idea. I'd set it up from the start, the Canine Cruise was my idea, because my cousin, Gerald, is one of the crew members who sets up the displays. He showed me how I could point the cannon and how to set it off with a timer. I had it set to go off at exactly 1:30 pm. It didn't take much to make sure that Melinda was in front of the camera and the canon at that time. But, again, I didn't intend for her to get hurt. It was just a childish practical joke, and one I regret whole-heartedly."

Colby's jaw tensed, his green eyes met Emma's for a moment before returning to the cameraman's. "You are claiming that the whole thing was just a practical joke then? Nothing else?"

Sean's eyes were wide. "Nothing else, I swear. I didn't mean for Melinda to be hurt."

The Adam's apple in Colby's neck bobbed up and down as he swallowed and met Emma's eyes again. She shrugged slightly enough for Colby to see, but hoped that the gentleman across the table wouldn't. Then Colby slid his gaze back to the two across the table. "Don't go anywhere when this ship meets port. Either of you. The Fairfax County Sheriff's office has already been appraised of the situation, and will want you both for further questioning in this. If Melinda dies, it makes no difference whether it was an accident or not, Mr. Rockfort. You'll be looking at being charged with at least manslaughter."

The color drained from Sean Rockfort's face as his gazed dropped to his hands.

Colby let out a slow breath. "And I'm going to need to see this video."

CHAPTER SIX

The blast of the confetti canon on the video recorder made Emma jump almost as much as she did when the incident had happened on the top deck. But what she realized as she watched the footage was that it had taken her more by surprise than it had Melinda, the reporter. It wasn't the pop that had made Melinda jump back, but the force of air from the gun pushing her toward the gate behind her, which had been unlatched, but still sat in place. So, Emma was unable to tell that there was anything wrong with the gate or that it was ajar in any way.

"Watch out!" a male voice yelled in the distance behind the camera, just before Melinda touched the gate and fell through the open hole. Her scream filled the air before she and her red dress disappeared over the edge.

Then the camera shot the floor of the deck as another voice yelled, "She can't swim!" just before the camera cut off.

Colby looked up at the two men sitting across the table from him. "Who yelled, 'watch out?'"

Both Sean and John looked at each other in confusion. Then they both looked back and shrugged. Sean answered, "I'm not really sure. I can't remember. It all happened so fast."

"I was in too much shock," John said with a frown, "I can't say it wasn't me."

Colby's brow furrowed. "It's hard to tell from the camera footage, but it would be good to know which of you did yell it. Could you both think a little harder, focus and try to remember?"

They both did, but to no avail. Neither of them could recall which had said it. It was an important piece of information in Emma's opinion, since the person who said it might have known that the gate was ajar. Then again, they may have just meant for her to not get to close to the railing in the first place. Emma wondered if she might just be reading too much into the situation. Perhaps she was trying too hard to find a clue that would point to the culprit, when it seemed obvious that the culprit had been Sean, who set up a practical joke that went horrifyingly wrong.

"Well, I'd prefer if you both remain here in the manager's office until we reach shore." Colby met eyes with both of them, and they each nodded in turn.

Then Colby turned and ushered Emma and Molly out of the room, closing the door behind all four of them. He leaned toward her. "Something didn't seem right about that video. Come on. Follow me upstairs, and we'll talk about it at the scene."

Emma nodded and followed.

Overhead, the gray clouds shifted, but the rain continued to hold off. The shoreline moved by quickly as the cruise ship continued up the Potomac, back to port. Emma stood on the top deck, seeing that the crew had cleared the left side of the ship, but didn't touch anything near where the accident had occurred. Everything remained as Colby and she had left it. And the metal gate continued to bang against the latch in the wind. Had it been windy earlier? She stepped close to the gate. "Do you think there will be fingerprints on the gate?"

Colby pushed his cap further on his head as he fought the wind. "I doubt it. The culprit wouldn't be dumb enough to do that, I'd think. He'd be more likely to step on the catch and then grab hold of the gate with his jacket sleeve. That's how I would do it."

"Like this?" Emma pulled her jacket sleeve down and grabbed hold of the other side of the metal gate. She pulled it over toward her, stepped on the latch lightly and then set it up so that it was flush with the rest of the rail across, but not completely latched. She stepped back from it. "It looks like it's latched, doesn't it?"

With a grim frown, Colby nodded. He stepped forward, covering his hand with the long sleeve of his ruby shirt and then lightly shoving on the gate. It flew open with barely a push. "It doesn't take much pressure for the gate to fly open, either, in this state."

"I wondered two things again as we watched the video," Emma said, rubbing her hands into the fur on Molly's head to warm them. "The person who yelled 'watch out' couldn't have been talking about this gate unless he knew it would fly open and either wanted the reporter to avoid it, or he wanted to keep himself from being implicated in the 'accident.'"

"That seems about right," Colby said, wrapping and unwrapping his leather leash around his hand in a nervous habit. "But neither of the men would admit to saying it or point the finger at the other. Do you think it's possible that they both are in on this?"

Emma did a half-shrug and a half-shake of the head. "I don't know. I don't think so though. Otherwise, why would John tell us about the practical joke at all?"

After a moment of quiet as the wind blew about them, Colby asked, "What was the second thing?"

She blinked at him. "Second thing?"

"You said there were two things you noticed after watching the video."

"Oh!' She stopped for a minute, looking up at him sheepishly before continuing, "I'm not sure if it's anything at all. It might be just me reading into it."

"Go ahead and tell me what you saw, and we'll decide if it's just you or if you see something worth taking note of."

She nodded. "It's just that the reporter had this look on her face right when the confetti cannon went off. It was like an 'I got you look.' It gave me the impression that the canon didn't surprise her at all, like maybe she even expected it."

His eyes went wide as he nodded. "I think you're right. I got the same impression."

Relief prickled across Emma's skin. "Then I think I know who the culprit is, and it's not both of them."

CHAPTER SEVEN

E mma and Colby stood in front of the two in the manager's office, ready to attempt to get a confession out of the culprit. Emma stood at the doorway of the office holding both Gabby's and Molly's leashes, blocking the escape should the culprit attempt to leave the room. Emma could never do it on her own, but Colby had told her the commands to get Gabby to both growl or attack if necessary. She replayed those words in her head a few times so she wouldn't forget them.

"After going through the evidence," Colby said, setting his phone on the table in front of the two men again to record the conversation, "We've determined that this accident was indeed staged and malicious—premeditated murder."

The two men's mouths dropped open, and the color drained from Sean's face. He shook his head emphatically. "I promise that it was just a joke. I didn't intend for Melinda to get hurt or fall over the edge of the railing. I had no idea that the gate was open or faulty. My cousin can back me up on this. The cannon didn't even shoot in the direction it was supposed to. Somehow it was in front of her instead of behind her. If anything, she should have tripped forward, face-first into the camera, not backward. And the cannon was set on high. Neither I nor Gerald set it on high."

Colby lifted a brow. "I believe you, Mr. Rockfort."

The cameraman blinked and leaned back in his chair, his brow suddenly furrowing. "Then what do you mean?"

"We believe that the victim knew about the practical joke. She intended to play it off and not act surprised at all. You wanted her to lose her composure, but instead, she intended to use it to her advantage, and prove to you that she was not the jumpy woman you thought she was."

"What? How?"

Colby turned on the man in the brown suit. "Mr. Truman, you told Melinda about the practical joke, didn't you?"

The manager in the brown suit lifted a brow. "What gives you that idea?"

"On the video footage, the reporter didn't look the least bit surprised when the cannon went off. It was the blast of wind that sent her backwards as the cannon was set on full blast. She wasn't surprised as much as she was pushed in the direction of the faulty railing. You had changed the location of the practical joke slightly and pointed the cannon in such a way that it would blast directly at the reporter, isn't that right, Mr. Truman?"

The man shook his head and smirked. "Of course it's not. Is the police into writing fiction, now?"

"Do your dress shoes have black soles, Mr. Truman?"

Slowly, the man nodded, his eyes narrowing on Colby.

"There is a black scuff mark on the gate's latch, proving that the last person to press the latch had on black soles."

Mr. Truman huffed. "I'm sure I'm not the only person aboard the ship who has black soles on their shoes."

Colby lifted a brow. "You're right, there, but Emma and I overheard you talking with the victim just as the boat began this journey. We got the distinct impression you were warning her about the very practical joke that was coming up in order to get her to change the position of the cannon herself."

The man crossed his arms over his chest. "This is a nice story, but what proof do you have?"

"I'm certain if we check the cannon for prints, we will find a set of prints matching the victim's. You told her about the practical joke because you overheard Sean talking to his cousin about it. You set the cannon on high and then you told the victim so that she would aim the cannon toward herself, in a new direction. Only she didn't know about the power of the blast of air from the cannon. Nor did she know about the gate that had been propped open behind her."

The man sat there, frowning, but glanced up once toward Emma as though gauging his ability to blow past her like a football linebacker. She swallowed and gripped the leashes tighter.

"Both of you knew about her inability to swim, and the Potomac is a fast moving river. Even the most experienced swimmer would struggle against the currents. And the boat was moving away from her, making it very likely that she would succumb to hypothermia before being rescued regardless."

Mr. Truman's hands fisted as he set them on his knees and leaned forward in his chair. "This still doesn't prove that it's my fault."

Slowly, Colby shook his head and set Emma's cell phone next to his on the table. "I've informed the doctor that I need the victim to call me the moment she wakes. When she does, I believe she'll be able to corroborate exactly what I just said. That you told her to change the direction of the cannon, herself. That you set up the place where the cannon was located and the scene would be shot. That you had every opportunity to set up the gate exactly as I described, so that no one would be able to tell the gate was propped, because the gate aligned with the rest of the railing almost perfectly. And I believe that we can have that video footage analyzed so that we can discover that it was you who called, 'watch out' just before she hit the railing, because you wanted it to be clear that you were far enough away from the scene of the accident for witnesses."

The point of the man's jaw moved in and out of his temple as he sat there, fuming and grinding his teeth. Sean continued to look back and forth between Colby and Mr. Truman in wide-eyed disbelief. Suddenly, Mr. Truman stood quickly enough that his chair flew behind him and hit the wall. Both Molly and Gabby jumped to their feet. Gabby growled.

"That heartless witch. She didn't deserve to live. My sister-in-law is in the hospital because of her, and my brother just shot himself this morning. He's dead! And she was unapologetic. Unsympathetic. My wife and I are going to be stuck raising their baby, because Sean, here, is a drunk. I had to take action. I couldn't just let her get away with all of this." Foam formed at the corners of Mr. Truman's mouth. "She deserved everything she got. I hope she dies and never wakes up."

Sean blinked at him, eyes wide.

Colby cleared his throat, pulling his handcuffs from his belt loop. "Then you got your wish, Mr. Truman. I already got word that the victim passed away soon after arriving at the hospital."

CHAPTER EIGHT

Emma leaned against her SUV listening the seagulls cry above her head. Gabby and Molly both leaned against her legs much like they had when she'd been standing against the door on the cruise ship earlier. The wind blew hard against her side, but the dogs helped her feel warmer. Almost as warm as the look Colby gave her as he approached after helping the Fairfax County deputy put the culprit, Mr. Truman, into the patrol car.

"You're incredible. You know that?" he asked as he drew near, his smile flashing the dimple in his left cheek while his green eyes sparkled. He rubbed the top of her head, just like he always had, since she was a kid, and then took the leash from her hand.

His words had made her heart soar momentarily... until his gesture of brotherly affection went and ruined the moment. She let out a slow sigh. "I didn't do very much."

He shook his head. "You are always noticing everything. It's like you have a superpower for noticing details that everyone else would overlook. I didn't even remember that that guy had said something to the reporter like that until you reminded me. And your mind worked together the details of the scene into what could have happened, and from the culprit's reaction, you were exactly right. We've got it all recorded on my phone, too."

Emma shrugged. "Like being obsessive compulsive about details and constantly anxious enough to think of every scenario is a good thing."

He huffed and then wrapped an arm around her shoulders, pulling her into a chaste hug that only lasted a moment. Not long enough, in Emma's opinion. Just long enough to feel the warmth she wanted to spend the rest of her life in before it was taken away from her. Just long enough for her to get a whiff of his spicy, cinnamon scent. "There's nothing wrong with you," he said. "You're perfect just as you are."

Butterflies tangled themselves in her stomach, and heat rose to her cheeks. She didn't know what to say, as she was struck completely dumb.

He smiled at her again as he took a step backwards. "I'll see you next week when I get back from the conference. I wanted to grab dinner with you tonight, but I've gotta head to the sheriff's office here in Fairfax to help process Mr. Truman. Drive safe, and I'll take you to dinner when Gabby and I get back to Ridgeway."

Emma nodded, swallowed down the lump in her throat and said, "Is that a promise?"

Colby laughed and continued walking backwards. "Yes, it's a promise. And text me when you get back, too, so I know you made it home safe."

She smiled. "I will."

Giddiness added a bit of spring to Colby's step as he made his way to his SUV. Emma brought Molly around the back of her truck and opened the hatch to let Molly jump in the back area. Once the Saint Bernard puppy was up at that level, she handed the dog one of the small treats from the bag she'd gotten from the vendor on the ship. Then she leaned forward and gave Molly a big hug, burying her hands in the white and brown fur, feeling the warmth of the puppy's body against her fingertips. Emma felt melancholy but hopeful. When she pulled away, she rubbed the top of Molly's head. "Is it silly to look forward to a dinner date, knowing that it's not a 'real' date?"

Molly lurched forward and licked Emma's cheek. Emma scrunched her nose and wiped the slobber away.

"Thanks. At least I know someone loves me," she said with a laugh as she stepped back and closed the hatch on her SUV.

A horn bonked lightly at her, and she whipped her head toward the sound. Even though Colby was in a hurry to get to the sheriff's office, he waved at her from his vehicle. He was obviously waiting for her to get in and start her truck, to make sure she got on the road safely. His gentlemanly manners warmed her heart again. Maybe what they had wasn't yet the kind of love that Emma really wanted, but for now she'd be happy that Colby at least cared about her this much.

The End

Look for more of Emma and Molly's adventures:
http://amazon.com/author/pcreeden

It's New Year's Eve and 20-year-old Emma Wright has a date with her crush—well, not a real date, but she can dream! Colby Davidson, the K9 search and rescue deputy, is allowing her to accompany him while he's on patrol at the Ridgeway Illumination Festival. Though they are just friends, she's still hoping for a possible kiss at the end of the festivities.

When a stranger asks them to help take some pictures at the event, Emma and Colby are happy to oblige. But their assistance turns them into alibis for the man's whereabouts while his girlfriend was killed. Most of the clues point to a robbery gone bad, but Emma doesn't believe all of them point that way. Was it really a robbery or was it murder?

It's Valentine's Day and 20-year-old Emma Wright just wants her crush to take notice of her. But Colby Davidson, the K9 search and rescue deputy only thinks of her as a kid sister. How will she get him to take her seriously?

When her veterinarian boss calls her to pick up a cat at a potential crime scene, she finds herself at the house of the richest woman in Ridgeway. Her father—the sheriff—and Colby are there. They both dismiss the untimely death as a heart attack, but Emma finds clues that it might be something more. Did the software billionaire die of natural causes, or was it murder?

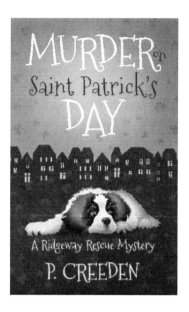

It's St. Patrick's Day and 20-year-old Emma Wright is working hard at training five-month-old Molly, her foster puppy, to become a therapy dog. But her training coach and neighbor gets an emergency call, cutting the lesson short, and Emma volunteers to pick up her daughter at a St. Patrick's Day concert in town.

When Emma arrives, the concert has just finished up, and the teenage girls are visiting with the band. Then the lead singer stumbles and falls to the ground, dead. Emma becomes the only level head in the crowd and calls for help. When the Sheriff and Colby arrive, they investigate it as a potential accident. But Emma finds subtle clues that something more sinister is going on. Did the leader of the band die in an accident, or was it murder?

Coming in May: Emma and Molly attend a wedding... where a murder

overcomes the romance of the occasion!

ABOUT THE AUTHOR

If you enjoyed this story, look forward to more books
by P. Creeden.
In 2019, she plans to release more than six
new books!
Hear about her newest release, FREE books when
they come available, and giveaways hosted by the
author—subscribe to her newsletter:
https://www.subscribepage.com/pcreedenbooks
All subscribers also get downloadable copy of
my PUPPY LOVE coloring book.

If you enjoyed this book and want to help the
author, consider leaving a review at your favorite
book seller – or tell someone about it on social
media. Authors live by word of mouth!

Manufactured by Amazon.ca
Acheson, AB

15276880R00037